ANTHEM

Ayn Rand

This edition published by Spark Publishing

Spark Publishing
A Division of SparkNotes LLC
120 Fifth Avenue, 8th Floor
New York, NY 10011

Printed and bound in the United States

ISBN 1-58663-825-4

Introduction: Stopping to Buy SparkNotes on a Snowy Evening

Whose words these are you *think* you know.
Your paper's due tomorrow, though;
We're glad to see you stopping here
To get some help before you go.

Lost your course? You'll find it here.
Face tests and essays without fear.
Between the words, good grades at stake:
Get great results throughout the year.

Once school bells caused your heart to quake
As teachers circled each mistake.
Use SparkNotes and no longer weep,
Ace every single test you take.

Yes, books are lovely, dark, and deep,
But only what you grasp you keep,
With hours to go before you sleep,
With hours to go before you sleep.

Contents

Context

AYN RAND WAS BORN in St. Petersburg, Russia, in February 1905, and grew up in Russia during one of the country's most tumultuous periods. Socialist revolutionaries overthrew the monarchy in 1905, and in 1906 the first Duma, the new Russian congress, convened. Several different socialist groups emerged after the revolution of 1905, chief among them the Bolsheviks and the Mensheviks. Several groups of revolutionaries fell to infighting, especially during World War I, in which the Bolsheviks urged an international civil war to bring about the rule of the proletariat, or governance by the working class. The country fell into a bitter civil war. The Bolsheviks, under Lenin, eventually emerged as the preeminent party, and the group later became the Communist Party.

In 1917, when she was twelve, Rand witnessed the Bolshevik Revolution, in which the Bolsheviks took control of the Soviet government, ushering in the Communist era in Russia. Her family lost its business and was reduced to a state of extreme poverty during the new regime. Rand despaired of the corrupt Communist system, which claimed to subjugate the needs of the individual to the needs of the many, but was ultimately manipulated by a few greedy and tyrannical leaders, with disastrous consequences for Russia's economy and people.

Rand completed high school in the Crimea, where she had fled to escape the civil war. She returned to St. Petersburg (then called Petrograd), where she attended the University of Petrograd, and she graduated in 1924 with a degree in philosophy and history. She also studied screenwriting at the State Institute for Cinema Arts.

After Joseph Stalin ascended to power in the early 1920s, a disillusioned and disgusted Rand escaped to Chicago in 1926. She then moved to Hollywood to pursue a career as a screenwriter. In Hollywood, she met her husband-to-be, actor Frank O'Connor, whom she married in 1929. Rand and O'Connor remained married until his death fifty years later. In 1932, Rand sold her first screenplay, *Red Pawn,* and her first stage play was produced on Broadway. The play, *Night of January 16th,* was a largely autobiographical account of the Soviet Union just after the revolution. She completed her first novel, *We the Living,* in 1933, and it was first published in 1936.

Anthem, Rand's second work of fiction, was first published in Great Britain in 1938. She later revised the novella and, in 1946, published it in the United States. According to the preface she wrote for the American edition, the only differences between the two editions were stylistic. In the American version, Rand sought to eliminate poetic and flowery language and to simplify and clarify the themes she laid out.

Rand is best known for her two longest works of fiction, *The Fountainhead* (1943) and *Atlas Shrugged* (1957). She began work on *The Fountainhead* in 1935, at the same time she was working on *Anthem.* Both works introduce her theory of objectivism, or egoism, the idea that an individual's worth comes from him- or herself and not from what he or she contributes to society or to mankind. Objectivism is, as both *The Fountainhead* and *Anthem* make explicit, a wholesale rejection of the collectivist theories and tactics that Rand believed were at the center of the brutalities visited on Russia during the early part of the twentieth century. While *The Fountainhead* is the fictional embodiment of objectivism, *Anthem* is Rand's political manifesto. It takes the form of an allegory, a fictional story whose purpose is to present a philosophical idea. *Anthem* describes a dystopia, a nightmarish imaginary world through which Rand speculates on the eventual result of society's negative aspects. Rand uses the dystopia to show what she believes will happen when a nation or society embraces collectivism and community ideals.

The novella largely mirrors the state of the Soviet Union under the Stalinist terror, during which Stalin ordered purges of all those who opposed him, especially independent thinkers and intellectuals. In her novels, Rand idealizes those of the sort Stalin executed and exalts her hero, a vibrant, intelligent, and physically beautiful youth, who fights his way through the nameless, faceless mass of society that seeks to use him for its own ends while draining him of all vitality and vigor. She rejects religion and group identity in favor of ego and self-determination.

Many consider *Atlas Shrugged,* which Rand began in 1946 and first published in 1957, to be her greatest accomplishment as a fiction writer. It is her longest and most elaborate novel, and it was her last fictional work. In the novel, she traces the lives of several individuals who are involved in big business in the United States, exalting their will to succeed and self-centered egoism. *Atlas Shrugged* fleshes out the philosophy Rand had been developing all her life, the beginnings of which are introduced in the concluding chapters of *Anthem*. The world depicted in *Atlas Shrugged* is modeled closely on America in the 1890s, during the height of free markets and governmental nonintervention in business.

After the publication of *Atlas Shrugged,* Rand wrote and lectured on objectivism. She died on March 6, 1982. Her books have garnered her a cult following of philosophers and thinkers, who continue her pursuit of objectivism and egoism in the form of foundations and think tanks devoted to her work.

PLOT OVERVIEW

A YOUTH NAMED EQUALITY 7-2521, who has found a hidden tunnel and hides in it to write, knows his solitude violates all the laws of his society. Even though he does not feel guilt for his actions, he begs the forgiveness of the ruling Council. As he spends more time alone, he realizes that solitude suits him, and he begins to crave more and more time by himself. From his tunnel, Equality 7-2521 records episodes from his childhood. As a child, Equality 7-2521 wanted more than anything to be a scholar. He believed he was cursed with a terrific curiosity, which made him prefer some things to others and to prefer some people to others. He often fought with the boys at the Home of Students, and he was reprimanded by his teachers for being too smart and too tall. He tried to conform to the standard the others set, but no matter how hard he tried, he was smarter and quicker than they were. When the Council of Vocations assigned him to be a street sweeper instead of a scholar, he was pleased because it meant he could atone for the sins he had committed.

When he was ten, Equality 7-2521 saw the public execution of the Transgressor of the Unspeakable Word, who had discovered the word "I" and was burned to death in the town square as punishment for using the word. While he was burning, the Transgressor showed no pain but locked eyes with Equality 7-2521. Equality 7-2521 comes to believe that that moment anointed him as a disciple of the same crusade as the Transgressor.

Equality 7-2521 begins to conduct experiments and shortly discovers electricity. After many weeks of work, he successfully builds a lightbulb from the materials he finds in his tunnel. He decides that he must share his invention with the world and resolves to present it to the World Council of Scholars when it convenes that year in his city.

In the meantime, Equality 7-2521 has met the Golden One, a beautiful peasant girl who is proud and haughty. He knows it is wrong to do so, but he speaks to her when he gets the chance, and they immediately fall in love. One day, she offers him some water from her hands, and he drinks it, not understanding why this act makes him think of the Palace of Mating, where he and all other mature citizens are sent once a year to have sex.

Before he can show the lightbulb to the World Council, Equality 7-2521 accidentally returns late to the Home of the Street Sweepers, where he lives. When he refuses to tell his Home Council where he has been, he is thrown into the Palace of Corrective Detention. There he is tortured, but he still refuses to tell where he has been, because he wants to keep the lightbulb a secret until he gets to show it to the World Council. He remains incarcerated until the World Council convenes, when he breaks out of the Palace of Corrective Detention and goes to the World Council, expecting to be exonerated and reconciled with his brothers.

When Equality 7-2521 arrives and tells the World Council his story, however, the World Council rejects him out of fear and anger. It threatens to kill him and to get rid of his lightbulb. He cannot abide having his lightbulb destroyed, so he grabs his invention and flees the city. He runs to the Uncharted Forest where he discovers that he is free at last to do as he pleases.

A few days later, the Golden One appears. She has followed Equality 7-2521 into the woods. They vow to live together in peace and solitude. After they have been hiking for several days in the mountains, they find an abandoned house from the Unmentionable Times. The Golden One revels in the finery she finds in the house, and Equality 7-2521 consumes the library. He discovers the meaning of the word "I," and he vows to protect his home and from there launch a new race of men who will believe in individualism and the never-ending supremacy of the ego.

CHARACTER LIST

Equality 7-2521 A street sweeper, the protagonist of the novella. Equality 7-2521, who later renames himself Prometheus, believes in individualism and rejects the collectivist society around him. He is vain and self-centered, strong, beautiful, and intelligent. He is deeply curious and desires freedom to explore and think, and he is unafraid of the society of mindless drones around him. Equality 7-2521 represents the superiority of a singular intellect to the homogeneity of the masses, who cannot think for themselves and are indistinguishable from one another.

The Golden One A beautiful peasant with whom Equality 7-2521 falls madly in love. The Golden One demonstrates her subservience to Equality 7-2521 by allowing him to change her name from Liberty 5-3000 to the Golden One, and later, Gaea. The Golden One is proud and vain, strong and bitter. She loves Equality 7-2521 because he is different from most men around her. With him, she grapples with a desire to find the word "I" in order to express her love for him. The Golden One is relatively underdeveloped as a character, functioning mostly as the object of Equality 7-2521's affection.

The Transgressor of the Unspeakable Word A martyr for the word "I." The Transgressor of the Unspeakable Word suffers no pain as he is burned alive because he knows the meaning of individualism. His death foreshadows the suffering and exile of Equality 7-2521, and he represents the way to die properly, in Rand's view, for the cause of egoism.

International 4-8818 Equality 7-2521's only friend.
International 4-8818 views Equality 7-2521 as a
prophet. When he and Equality 7-2521 discover the
tunnel in which Equality 7-2521 hides to write his
journal and make his discoveries, he is torn between
loyalty to his friend and his desire not to break the law.
International 4-8818 represents the citizen who
secretly seeks his own meaning but is unable to realize
it because he cannot take the step of breaking with
his society.

Collective 0-0009 The leader of the World Council of Scholars.
Collective 0-0009 is shapeless and cowardly, like all
members of the World Council. He fears and hates
Equality 7-2521 for breaking the rules because he
believes that only those decisions reached by the
council can be of value. Collective 0-0009
represents the thinking force behind the evil
collectivism of the city.

ANALYSIS OF MAJOR CHARACTERS

EQUALITY 7-2521

Equality 7-2521 begins the novella as a benighted, if exceptional, youth, who has only barely realized that he might be different from those around him. He regrets his differences and tries to bring himself into conformity. His relationship with International 4-8818, his only friend, exemplifies the halfhearted attempts he makes to eliminate all his preferences for individual people, to care for each brother equally, and to be identical to his brothers. After the discovery of the tunnel, however, he realizes that solitude pleases him, and it becomes harder for him to deny his own individuality.

When Equality 7-2521 meets the Golden One, he no longer wants to deny that he prefers some of his peers to others. Because he wants to think about her all the time, and because the urge is so overwhelming, he gives himself to his sin. In so doing, he takes his first major step down the road toward breaking with society. Moreover, the Golden One represents Equality 7-2521's first meaningful encounter with another human being. His relationship with her baffles him. He knows that he wants to possess her, but he does not know why. He admires her haughtiness and her strength, and he knows she admires the same things in him, but he does not understand why his preference for her is so overpowering.

The discovery of the lightbulb pushes Equality 7-2521 into complete rebellion. He now has a cause for which he would give his life. Until the moment when the World Council threatens to destroy the lightbulb, Equality 7-2521 thinks of his brothers and their welfare. Because he will not abide seeing the lightbulb destroyed, even though he might tolerate his own destruction, he is forced into exile from his society. Equality 7-2521 realizes that he actually created the lightbulb for its own sake and that he does want to live because his body is strong and youthful and beautiful—a realization that severs his last connections to society and makes him a free man.

Once he has broken from society, Equality 7-2521 adopts a vanity and pride unknown in the society in which he was raised and, in so doing, he realizes his manhood. For the first time, Equality 7-2521 feels pride at killing his own food and pleasure in eating, and when he meets up again with the Golden One, he enjoys sex for the first time. The ecstasy he discovers in his body mirrors the ecstasy of his mind. By breaking from the confines of society, Equality 7-2521 becomes his own man in both his mind and his body.

The abandoned house in the forest represents Equality 7-2521's ability to provide for himself on a permanent basis. He is very proprietary about the house and its contents, and it provides the key to his epiphany. Upon discovering the "I" while he is reading in the library in the house, Equality 7-2521 suddenly becomes aware that he is the center of his own universe, and the curse he has been fighting is actually a blessing to be embraced. He realizes that he is an end in himself and that his happiness is reason enough to live. With this epiphany, his transformation is complete. He is unafraid and singular, self-important and proud. He has discovered himself and become his own man.

Rand intends Equality 7-2521's name to be ironic, since we know that Equality 7-2521 is far superior to his peers and does not believe in the doctrine of equality. His decision to discard his given name shows his frustration with his society, his unwillingness to be held back among the masses. In renaming himself Prometheus, Equality 7-2521 shows that he identifies himself with the bringer of light, fire, and progress in Greek mythology. He considers himself a hero who, like Prometheus, must defy the conventions of his time.

THE GOLDEN ONE

Though the Golden One undergoes several name changes, she herself is fairly static throughout the novella. From the beginning, she is haughty and proud, rejecting all society except Equality 7-2521, whom she adores from the outset because he is stronger and sharper than the rest of her brothers. She becomes subservient to him almost immediately, seeking to care for him as early as the third time they meet, when she provides him with water to cool himself. By the time she follows him into the forest, she has become totally his possession, and she remains that way until the end.

Although she is a static character, the Golden One does exhibit extraordinary curiosity when it comes to finding the "I" and her uncommon beauty. Though the only reason the Golden One seeks to say "I" is to tell Equality 7-2521 that she loves him, a far less noble goal than his effort at self-actualization, she is nevertheless superior to those around her because she at least suspects that there is more to the world than the collective equality enforced in her society. Additionally, she stands out from the faceless, nameless masses because she is incredibly beautiful, a sign from Rand, who views physical beauty as the natural counterpart to intellectual and personal integrity, that she is a good character in the novella. Despite the poor development of her character, then, we know quite a bit about the Golden One's attitude toward her culture and society, and her rejection of both is enough to exalt her in the novella to special status.

The Golden One is a problematic character, however, because her originality is at odds with her subservience to Equality 7-2521. On the one hand, she is the female counterpart to Equality 7-2521 in that she is curious and seeks solitude. For this reason, we might expect to read a considerable amount about her thoughts and reactions or conversation with Equality 7-2521. But the Golden One has almost no lines in the novella, and she fades into the background when Equality 7-2521 finally realizes his own self-importance. On the other hand, though she is Equality 7-2521's counterpart she totally abdicates control to him and is remarkably underdeveloped, especially considering that she is the only other consistently present character in the novella. Though her name is originally Liberty 5-3000, she allows Equality 7-2521 to rename her the Golden One and, later, Gaea. Her willingness to accept the new names that Equality 7-2521 gives her is a symptom of her broader willingness to accept the identity that he conceives for her. Her subservience and underdevelopment are troubling because in her character Rand presents the novella's only other example of goodness in a collective society. But because the Golden One has no personal characteristics of her own, she ultimately serves as a flat mirror to Equality 7-2521, revealing little about Rand's philosophy that we do not already glean from Equality 7-2521.

CHARACTER ANALYSIS

THEMES, MOTIFS & SYMBOLS

THEMES

Themes are the fundamental and often universal ideas explored in a literary work.

THE PRIMACY OF THE INDIVIDUAL

Equality 7-2521 realizes the significance of his existence only when he comes to understand that one is the center of one's universe, and that one's perception gives the world its meaning. He struggles throughout *Anthem* with his growing desire to spend time alone, to write for his own benefit only, and to create at his own leisure and for his own purposes. Only after his break with society, however, does Equality 7-2521 feel his own strength and ability. Alone, Equality 7-2521 thrives, even in the forest, where he initially expects to be destroyed by beasts. In society, all the brothers are drained of their energy and sapped of their creativity until they become shapeless, faceless blobs made inarticulate by fear of rejection by the group. By contrast, those characters capable of thinking on their own exhibit strength, fearlessness, and self-assurance. In his final epiphany, Equality 7-2521 declares his will the only edict he will obey and his happiness his only goal.

Rand writes *Anthem* as a warning to those who believe that collectivist societies, like the one whose birth she witnessed in Russia early in the twentieth century, can ever be successful. She warns that losing sight of the individual and his or her needs will lead to the destruction of all progress and all forward movement. Nevertheless, she believes that the individual can never really be dominated—he or she will always resurface because freedom is part of the human makeup. Rand believes that no matter how hard society tries and how many people it kills in the name of collectivism, the individual will still rise up and declare him- or herself his or her own purpose.

THE VALUE OF MARTYRDOM

Martyrdom sets Equality 7-2521 apart from the rest of society because, in Rand's view, the willingness to die for an ideal marks a hero and distinguishes him or her from the rest of society. Indeed, when society martyrs a hero, the hero feels nothing but joy at the discovery of his or her ideal. Thus, when he is burned at the stake in front of Equality 7-2521, the Transgressor of the Unspeakable Word shows no fear or pain, only tremendous elation in his knowledge of the word that the rest of society has forgotten. Likewise, when Equality 7-2521 is beaten in the Palace of Corrective Detention for refusing to tell his Home Council where he has been, he feels no pain, only joy that he has not revealed the secret of the lightbulb. He even consents to stay locked in his cell until it is time to break out and go to the World Council of Scholars. In both cases, what matters to the martyr is not the pain but the ideal, and the ideal is worth dying for, as Equality 7-2521 observes in his meditations in Chapter XII.

THE IMPOTENCE OF THE COLLECTIVE

The World Council of Scholars embodies one of the chief evils of collectivism—the inability of a collective government to come to a conclusion and take action on behalf of the society it governs. Because consensus is impossible and individual thinking forbidden, the council falls into inaction; since the council is the ruling body of the society, society stops advancing. The World Council of Scholars exemplifies the fear that controls group thinking. Because the council members cannot all agree on technological advances, even a simple innovation such as the candle takes a huge amount of time and haggling to gain approval. Moreover, because consensus-building is difficult and dangerous in a society in which discord is viewed as a sin, the individuals on the council begin to fear any change as a threat to themselves. For this reason, the council recoils from Equality 7-2521's lightbulb. Rand shows that when absolute agreement is necessary for change, progress is all but impossible.

ORIGINAL CREATION AS A COMPONENT OF IDENTITY

For Rand, a man's value rests in the originality of his mind as expressed in his work, and the value of his work resides in his personal investment in it, as in Equality 7-2521's invention of the lightbulb. Equality 7-2521 discovers in his tunnel that the work of an individual's hands is an extension of the individual's very self, and that the value of the product of this work lies not in the product's benefit for society but in its own existence as the fruit of the individual's imagination. For this reason, Equality 7-2521 prefers to be beaten into unconsciousness and then nearly starved to death than to reveal the light he has invented. Furthermore, when the World Council of Scholars rejects his light as useless, he tells the council members to do what they will with his body, if only they will accept the light. Last, when Equality 7-2521 and the Golden One finally reach the house, his proprietary sense over the building, which he refashions into a home for him and the Golden One, is so strong that he is willing to defend it even to the death. In each of these cases, Equality 7-2521 defends his work and his property as extensions of himself because they spring from him.

MOTIFS

Motifs are recurring structures, contrasts, or literary devices that can help to develop and inform the text's major themes.

FEAR

Fear in *Anthem* characterizes those social lepers who do not have enough sense of themselves to understand that each individual is the center of his or her universe. Rand's heroes, on the other hand, never fear anything. In Rand's belief system, the only thing man has to fear is his fellows, who will weigh him down and sap his strength if given the opportunity. The Golden One appeals to Equality 7-2521 because she is unafraid, and she is attracted to him for the same reason. By contrast, those in the Home of the Street Sweepers are so afraid that they do not speak to each other at dinner or in the sleeping hall. More generally, those in a society characterized by fear never seek to make any progress or improve their own lives. They do not show signs of individuality—they never exhibit vanity, pride, lust, or preference for some people over others—because they value physical safety over expressions of self.

NAMING

In the society in *Anthem,* naming is a form of identifying one's possessions as one's own. For this reason, Equality 7-2521 names the Golden One on two separate occasions, names himself, and searches relentlessly for the word "I." Rand alludes to the power of naming granted to Adam in the Bible, where he is made master of the animals and they answer to the names he gives them. Likewise, Rand's heroes rename those things that are dear to them. By contrast, those in society are given numbers and social concepts as identifying tags, as yet another way of stealing their individuality from them. For those in this society, possession is not a possibility because all things are owned by the collective, including their own bodies and identities. Thus, when Equality 7-2521 renames the Golden One and himself, he is declaring war on this philosophy and reclaiming himself and her as individuals.

SHAPELESSNESS

Like fear, shapelessness in *Anthem* connotes evil because it illustrates a lack of willingness or ability to believe in something and to stand behind it. For Rand, the physical world mirrors the internal, personal world, and physical shapelessness goes hand in hand with fear and collectivity. Thus, the members of the World Council of Scholars are all shapeless, as are the members of the Council of Vocations. The entire society around Equality 7-2521 is shapeless and gray, demonstrating its stagnation and worthlessness. By contrast, the Golden One is hard, with sharply defined lines and an overwhelming physical beauty. Similarly, International 4-8818 stands out among his peers because he is taller and more shapely than they are. Finally, Equality 7-2521 is reprimanded by his teachers at an early age for growing to more than six feet tall. The teachers, in keeping with the rigid norms of their society, try to enforce a uniformity that leads to shapelessness. That Equality 7-2521 does not fit in with this uniformity points him out as a true individual.

SYMBOLS

> *Symbols are objects, characters, figures, or colors used to represent abstract ideas or concepts.*

LIGHT

Light represents truth in *Anthem*. Thus, Liberty 5-3000 becomes the Golden One, and Equality 7-2521 becomes Prometheus, the bringer of light. Equality 7-2521's contribution to the world is his invention of the lightbulb, and the house he and the Golden One find in the forest has windows to let in the light. By contrast, the city is dingy and dark, and the only colors are gray, white, and brown. The whole society lives by candlelight, and the society's leaders fear the light when Equality 7-2521 brings it to them. Light illuminates human dignity and human error for Rand, both of which the society in *Anthem* tries to sweep under the rug. In the vast gray haze of this society, all things are indistinct. Only when light is brought to bear can those with exceptional qualities be differentiated from the crowd. Thus, Equality 7-2521's lightbulb makes him a harbinger of tremendous social unrest at the same time that it helps him see himself as the unique individual he really is.

THE FOREST

For Equality 7-2521, the state of nature affords him the chance to live alone and sustained by the work of his own hands, an opportunity he is denied in society. Unlike society, which constrains what an individual can claim as his own, the forest welcomes Equality 7-2521 and provides him what he needs. The forest is also a connection between the past and the future. In the forest, Equality 7-2521 and the Golden One find a new home for themselves—the only remnant of the Unmentionable Times in the story. This home suits them, and in it they discover their own natural states. The forest thus provides them with a place to effect their own rebirth.

MANUSCRIPTS

In the society in *Anthem,* manuscripts carry history and are sacred vessels for self-expression. The manuscripts that Equality 7-2521 steals from the Home of the Scholars are very important to him because they are his only means of recording his private thoughts. Because he is accustomed to believing that no thought is valid unless it is shared by the entire community, his willingness to record his thoughts, to see them as valuable, represents his first significant break with society. The books he finds in his new forest home are also important to him because they teach him the history of the old world's destruction and, most important, teach him the word "I." This discovery concludes Equality 7-2521's search for individual expression and allows him to think of himself as separate from the rest of his peers. It also teaches him a deeply personal kind of pleasure, both in the form of reading, which is itself a solitary activity in his life, and in writing, which allows him to speak so that only he can hear. Equality 7-2521's obsession with his manuscripts, then, reflects a deep-seated need to escape the prying eyes of the society around him and to realize his full potential as an individual.

Summary & Analysis

Introduction & Author's Preface

Summary: Introduction

Leonard Peikoff introduces the fiftieth anniversary edition of *Anthem* with a discussion of Ayn Rand's philosophy, objectivism. He discusses Rand's constancy as a political thinker and philosopher and her persistence in flouting the criticism of those who believed in socialism and responded to her work by saying that she did not understand socialism's tenets. He points to quotations from several of her letters to support the idea that she believed from a very young age in the primacy of the individual and the danger of collective ideals and social planning.

Peikoff discusses Rand's decision to change the title of the novel from *Ego,* its working title, to *Anthem,* a move he says was motivated by a purely artistic decision not to give away too much of the plot and philosophy before the reader had read the novella. He says Rand believed *Anthem* did not have a climax or plot in the traditional sense, but was instead a kind of anthem, an exploration of an understanding of the world and a coming to terms with this philosophy's rejection of general society. Peikoff characterizes objectivism as a way of resolving a conflict between facts and values—in other words, as a way of seeing the world for what it is while at the same time holding true to a moral ideal. He claims that Rand deliberately uses biblical language, even in the title, in order to turn on its head the idea that profound awe can be experienced only in the face of the supernatural.

Anthem was not immediately accepted by the American literary establishment, according to Peikoff, who chronicles in some detail Rand's efforts to get the novella published. He says American intellectuals were in the grip of Communist ideas at the time Rand wrote the work, and it took the recognition of two conservative publishing houses for it to gain an American following. Once it was published, however, it gained tremendous popularity. Rand originally conceived *Anthem,* according to Peikoff, as a play, later as a magazine serial, and finally, at the suggestion of her publisher, as a novella.

SUMMARY: AUTHOR'S PREFACE

Rand herself prefaces *Anthem* by exhorting collectivists, those who believe in uniting individual labor efforts under the auspices of the single government for the good of the whole, to acknowledge that they are forcing individuals into slavery. She asserts that social goals have become commonplace in society, and that it should be obvious to all people that the world is headed toward a complete disintegration of the kind she portrays in *Anthem*. She wants those who advocate such goals to be honest about their intentions, and where their intentions may lead, so that in the future, when the world completely yields to the ideals of the collective, and people find themselves slaves, they will not be able to deny that they chose their own paths.

Rand also is careful to emphasize that in this, the American edition of the novel, she has not changed any of *Anthem*'s substance. She notes that she has only clarified the language and not changed the spirit of the novella. She claims the idea of objectivism has always been clear and does not need any further examination.

Furthermore, Rand responds to criticism that *Anthem* is unfair to the ideals of collectivism. She points to the state of the world in 1946 to show that forced labor and co-opting the profits of the work of individuals are accepted and advocated practices. She claims that the world does in fact contain councils of the kind she describes in *Anthem*, and that if her novella seems exaggerated, it is only because the world has not yet totally fallen into collective despair. Nevertheless, she says, the world is headed for just such a collapse, and *Anthem* is meant to change the minds of those who believe that socialism can exist without leading directly to its logical conclusion. This conclusion, she believes, is the disembodiment of the individual, the boredom and fear of the citizenry, and the inability of society to reap the benefit of individual work and products.

ANALYSIS: INTRODUCTION & AUTHOR'S PREFACE

Leonard Peikoff, who worked closely with Ayn Rand for thirty years before her death, is one of the world's leading Rand scholars, and his introduction is typical of the writing of most objectivist scholars. His intense, clipped style and self-assured tone are characteristic of both Rand herself and those who continue to propagate her ideas. Unlike many authors, Rand saw herself largely as a political figure and philosopher, though she believed the ideas she espoused were universal and eternal. Objectivism, though often spoken of by its followers as anti-religious, is similar to religion in the sense that it is an all-encompassing philosophy that views every fact in the world through a particular lens. Rand embraced this idea wholly, and her tone and style convey an absolute surety and confidence in her ideas that set her apart from many other novelists, especially those in twentieth-century America. Rand does not pose a question about society; she presents the answer. Peikoff and Rand's emphasis on the similarities of the two editions of *Anthem* underscore their interest in presenting objectivism and Rand as constant and unwavering in the face of enormous resistance from the intellectual community.

Peikoff's observations about the lack of traditional structure in *Anthem* are important to understanding how the novella works as a whole and what Rand was trying to accomplish with publication of the work. Though *Anthem* is plainly fictional, it is less like a novel and more like a manifesto, or statement of views. It does not, for example, contain detailed descriptions of characters or setting, or have easily identifiable structural components, such as a climax. Rather, it seeks to compel us to fear what Rand considers the error of embracing collectivism and to stave off this future by embracing the tenets of objectivism.

CHAPTER I

SUMMARY

Always referring to himself as "we," a youth named Equality 7-2521 writes in a journal from underground, where he is alone in an abandoned railroad tunnel. He and his friend International 4-8818 discovered the tunnel when they were working as street sweepers behind the theater near the edge of the unnamed city where they live. Equality 7-2521, ignoring International 4-8818's objections that it is forbidden because the Council has not allowed it, goes down into the tunnel to explore. He concludes that the tunnel must have been built by men during the Unmentionable Times of long ago, and it must therefore be an evil place. Nonetheless, he is drawn to the train tracks that he finds there, and when he reemerges from the hole, he makes International 4-8818 promise not to tell anyone about the hole. International 4-8818, an artist who is strong and funny, is very upset by this idea because it might be forbidden, but out of a sense of loyalty to Equality 7-2521, he agrees, though even the sense of loyalty that he feels upsets him because preference of one person over another is not permitted by the Council.

After he finds the tunnel, Equality 7-2521 returns to it each night by sneaking away from the group home where he lives when the others all go to the theater for the nightly show. He has stolen candles from the Home of the Street Sweepers and manuscripts from the Home of the Scholars. He writes and thinks alone in the tunnel. He acknowledges that his being alone is evil, considering the desire to be alone a part of his curse, but he feels no shame or regret about it. He very much enjoys talking to himself and for his own ears, even though he has been taught that it is evil to do anything for oneself. He knows that if he is discovered he will be punished harshly.

Equality 7-2521 describes his childhood at the Home for Infants, where he lived with all the other boys of his age, in a white room with a hundred beds and nothing else in it. At the age of five, he moved to the Home of the Students, where he lived until he was fifteen. He was a troublesome child because he often fought with the other boys who lived there. His teachers disliked him because he was too smart, and the authorities chastised him because he was taller than the others. He tried to be like the other children, but his curse kept him from achieving normalcy. He especially tried to be like Union 5-3992, a dull and stupid boy in his class. His curse made him curious and pushed him to ask questions, which his teachers eventually forbade.

When he turned fifteen, Equality 7-2521, like all the other boys, was assigned his task for the remainder of his life by the Council of Vocations. Equality 7-2521 desperately wanted to be assigned to the Home of the Scholars, who develop all technology for the society, including the candle, the most recent invention, discovered a century earlier. He wanted to be a scholar more than anything, even more than being a leader, a status considered a great honor in his society, allowing those so assigned to live in the Home of the Leaders, the largest building in the city. Equality 7-2521 sinned by wanting, however, and he was pleased to be able to make restitution for his sin by embracing his assigned profession—street sweeper.

In the tunnel, Equality 7-2521 records in his journal how he had lived at the Home of the Street Sweepers for four years, leading the highly structured life of a street sweeper, when he discovered the tunnel with International 4-8818 and began writing his journal.

ANALYSIS

Equality 7-2521 is Rand's prophet, in the sense that he rejects all the collectivism that has come before him and ushers in a new age of individualism. His society rejects him because he is superior to it, both intellectually and physically, and, most important for Rand, in his belief that the self is important. A few are drawn to his superiority, in spite of the masses' scorn. International 4-8818, though he cannot comprehend why he feels such tremendous loyalty to his friend, is nevertheless compelled to stand by him, in defiance of everything his society has taught him. In this way, International 4-8818 operates as Equality 7-2521's disciple, following him and believing him, even though he does not understand why he does so. Moreover, we are alerted to the importance of International 4-8818's devotion through the use of dialogue, a rare occurrence in the novella.

The comparison between Equality 7-2521 and traditional Judeo-Christian prophets is far from perfect, however. Although the language and the plot of the novella contain countless references to allegories from the lives of Christ and Moses and the story of Genesis, Equality 7-2521 does not reference a higher being and does not claim to come in the name of the higher power. Instead of worshipping a god of any kind, Equality 7-2521 worships himself. On the other hand, Equality 7-2521 is similar to other prophets in the sense that everything that came before is modified in light of the message he bears. Though he has been taught to believe that being alone and worshipping the self are sins, he feels no regret about doing these things because he believes them to be right, which is more important to him than anything society can teach him.

Although Rand makes many allusions to actual historical details about life in Soviet Russia, *Anthem* is removed from any particular historical setting and placed in a kind of every-country, an unnamed future world in which individual needs are ignored in favor of the common good. Thus, the references to the Councils and to the nightly meetings at the City Theatre bear close resemblance to the state of affairs in the Soviet Union in the early twentieth century, but the total regression of all technology is an exaggeration that is not grounded in historical fact. By separating the novella from the Soviet Union, Rand makes the story a warning to all people. The novella does not just announce the dangers of adopting Russian socialism, under which many people blamed specific corruptions for the atrocities that were committed in the name of the common good.

It also blames the very idea of collectivism for the demise of the human race. Rand believes that this destruction is inevitable where men come to believe in social planning, not just in the case of the specific evils of communist Russia. Although *Anthem* certainly makes reference to the problems plaguing Russia at the time of its publication, the work is more than just an invective against Lenin, who inaugurated the communist era in Russia, or Stalin, who carried out horrifying purges against the intellectual elite in the name of the good of the many.

In the opening chapter, Rand sets up the images that occur throughout the novella to draw our attention to the values she is promoting. The most important element of this imagery is the contrasted pairs she sets up. These pairings point us toward the characters and scenarios she believes are good and those she believes are evil. For example, the dark and dingy tunnel is lit by a candle but Equality 7-2521 prefers it to the pristine white of the homes in which he has lived with all his fellow infants, students, and street sweepers. Additionally, the villains of the novella are soft, featureless, and dead-seeming, like the members of the Council of Vocations, while the hero and later the heroine are hard and strong and vibrant. Indeed, in most cases, Rand turns traditional images on their heads by making the dark and hard preferable to the light and gentle.

The worst part of the collective society for Rand is its bland obliteration of all individual characteristics and features. Thus, Equality 7-2521, the hero, is taller than his compatriots, and International 4-8818, who is also a good character, stands apart from his fellows because he has laughter in his eyes. These features mark the good characters, while the villains are indistinguishable from one another. Indeed, throughout the story, the physical world closely models the internal world, and what is good can be seen as good from the outside as well as from what Rand reveals of the inside.

CHAPTER II

*There was no pain in their eyes and no knowledge of
the agony of their body. There was only joy in them,
and pride, a pride holier than it is fit for human pride
to be.* (See QUOTATIONS, p. 49)

SUMMARY

Equality 7-2521 meets Liberty 5-3000, a worker in the Home of the
Peasants. She is working in the fields near the road he is sweeping
when he sees her and falls in love with her. She is physically beautiful, tall, and blonde with a hard face and an unafraid expression.
She sees him on the road, and the next day, she comes over to the
hedges where he is working. They do not speak to each other but
gesture so each recognizes the other. He comes to name Liberty 5-
3000 the Golden One.

Several days later, Equality 7-2521 and the Golden One speak
for the first time. He tells her that she is beautiful, and she remains
stoic upon receiving the compliment. She tells him she does not want
him to be her brother, and he tells her that he does not want her to be
his sister. On the second day, while they are looking at each other,
Equality 7-2521 thinks of the City Palace of Mating, a place where
all the physically mature men and women of the city are sent each
year and assigned to have sex with another person. Equality 7-2521
does not understand why he thinks of the City Palace of Mating
while he is looking at the Golden One, but he does not want to see
her there. Fortunately, the Golden One is only seventeen, not old
enough to be sent to the City Palace of Mating. Nevertheless, the
thought makes Equality 7-2521 very angry, and the Golden One
sees his anger and smiles. In "the wisdom of women" she under-
stands more than Equality 7-2521.

At dinner, Equality 7-2521 is reprimanded for singing out of joy.
He tells the reprimanding Council Member that he is happy and that
is why he sings, and the Council Member tells him that he should be
happy since he lives among his brothers. In the tunnel, Equality 7-
2521 meditates on the meaning of happiness and the fact that it is
forbidden to be unhappy. He concludes that his brothers are not
happy because they are afraid. Equality 7-2521 is not afraid when
he is in his tunnel, and he concludes that he wishes not to be afraid,
that he is glad to live, even though his lack of fear arouses suspicion
in his brothers. He notices Fraternity 2-5503, who sobs and cries

without explanation, and Solidarity 9-6347, who has screaming fits in the middle of the night.

Equality 7-2521 begins to dream of the Unmentionable Times and the Uncharted Forest, which has overgrown the cities of that time. He begins to wonder what the Evil Ones, those who lived in the Unmentionable Times, thought and wrote, about whom only those in the Home of the Useless still have any memory. He wonders about the Unspeakable Word, which used to be present in the language of men but is not anymore. Speaking the Unspeakable Word is the only crime punishable by death. He recalls seeing the Transgressor of the Unspeakable Word burned alive in the town square for speaking the Unspeakable Word, and he remembers that there was no pain in his face, only joy. As he died, the Transgressor of the Unspeakable Word stared at Equality 7-2521, and Equality 7-2521 thought he looked like a saint.

ANALYSIS

In the Golden One, Equality 7-2521 finds a match for his physical perfection and stoic self-righteousness. Though she later bows to Equality 7-2521 as her master, Rand introduces the Golden One here as the pinnacle of feminine power and wisdom. The Golden One takes Equality 7-2521's affection for her as a personal triumph, and she is hard and unafraid like him. He worships her and thinks of her constantly as a goal to be achieved and an object to be admired. Even once they meet, their encounters are discreet, and he comes to her as an admirer, while she in turn accepts his admiration as the natural conclusion of her perfection. Feminists criticize Rand's view of women, arguing that it idealizes and dehumanizes them and ultimately subjugates them to the will of men. Rand, however, believes that the success of women is in their innate wisdom—an unspoken, intuitive kind of knowledge—and in their physical beauty. As with all her characters, Rand idealizes physical beauty, which sets her heroes apart from her villains.

Sex and the relationship between men and women play an important role in Rand's works, including *Anthem,* in which she presents the City Palace of Mating as the ultimate evil in sexual relations because is allows for sex without choice. Notably, Equality 7-2521 does not even recognize the connection between his love for the Golden One and his physical lust, and he feels shame at the idea that he could be forced to have sex with the Golden One or to witness her be forced to have sex with someone else. For Rand, sex is not sex without choice, and so there is no connection at all between the City Palace of Mating and the pure love felt by Equality 7-2521 for the Golden One.

Equality 7-2521's meditations on happiness involve fear and freedom, a contrast that runs throughout *Anthem*. For Rand, happiness is possible only with absolute freedom, and freedom erases all possibility of fear. Fear accompanies the introduction of arbitrary power into human existence, epitomized by the forcing of individuals to work for the good of others. The Transgressor of the Unspeakable Word is another example of the impossibility of fear in the face of freedom. Though he is burned on the pyre, he is unafraid of death or torture because he has learned to speak of himself as "I." Rand does not explicitly say why the Transgressor is not afraid, but his bravery can be explained by the fact that Rand's philosophy holds that individualism brings great happiness and that it is worth dying to experience one's own sense of self. Though the Transgressor's death, of course, mirrors the tales of Judeo-Christian saints and martyrs, the nature of his martyrdom contrasts with the nature of theirs. In Christian stories, the saints suffer on earth, even as they die, in the knowledge that they will be rewarded for their suffering with heaven. They firmly hold the ideal for which they are martyred, but the martyrdom itself is torturous. For Rand, by contrast, true happiness and ideals are possible on earth, and so death in the name of an ideal is its own reward. Her characters do not suffer for their faith; rather, their faith provides their happiness.

The discussion of the Unmentionable Times alerts us to the fact that this is not a society that has failed to achieve greatness but rather one that has forgotten that which made it great. This difference is important, as the existence of this past provides Equality 7-2521 with a glimpse of an alternative model for society and for his own existence. Rand does not specify how long before Equality 7-2521's time this fall from greatness occurred, but it occurred recently enough that the people in the Home of the Useless still recall the old times and that Equality 7-2521 knows that the Uncharted Forest was not always there—that it sprung up over the old cities. The knowledge of this past gives Equality 7-2521 something to aspire to, and his growing obsession with the Unmentionable Times foreshadows his eventual break from the society that constrains him.

CHAPTERS III–IV

SUMMARY: CHAPTER III

While dissecting a frog hanging on a copper wire, Equality 7-2521 discovers the power of electricity, which he explores in his tunnel underground. In his journal, he recounts his experiments: he makes a magnet move using electricity and creates a lighting rod outside the tunnel. He explores his tunnel to look for technology, and he discovers unidentified boxes with wires and switches and lightbulbs, although he does not yet know how to use them. He worries that he is the only person in the world with this knowledge because he has been taught that the Council of Scholars knows everything and that all men share all collective knowledge. Along these lines of thinking, anything known by only one person cannot be true by virtue of the fact that not everyone knows it.

At first Equality 7-2521 says that he has discovered a new power that was previously unknown to any man. This power frightens him even though he believes it is a very important and potent force. Later, Equality 7-2521 concludes that electricity is the power of the sky, and that men in the Unmentionable Times had harnessed the power of the sky. He becomes an avid scientist, exploring the power of electricity, and in his quest he realizes how much he does not know and how much of his previous learning had been mistaken. Equality 7-2521 announces in his journal that he knows more than the Council of Scholars, something which his society believes is impossible.

SUMMARY: CHAPTER IV

Many days after his first conversation with the Golden One, Equality 7-2521 speaks to her again by the hedges along the road he sweeps. She is waiting for him there when he arrives one afternoon, and he sees that she will obey him, despite her scorn for the rest of the world. He tells her that he has renamed her "the Golden One," and she tells him that she has renamed him "the Unconquered." He warns her that such thoughts are not permitted, and she responds that he thinks them anyway and wants her to think them. He agrees, but, calling her "dearest one," warns her not to obey him. He believes he is the first man ever to call a woman "dearest one." She offers her body to him in submission by gesturing that she belongs to him.

The Golden One urges Equality 7-2521 to come into the field where it is cooler, but he refuses to cross the hedge, so she brings him

water to drink. She holds the water in her hands and holds her hands to his lips, and they stand that way for several moments after he has finished drinking. Even though their conversation remains undiscovered by the others in the field, they each back away, confused by their intimate gesture.

ANALYSIS: CHAPTERS III–IV

Equality 7-2521's break with society manifests itself in both explicit and more subtle, structural ways. With the discovery of electricity, Equality 7-2521 moves away from his musings on the state of his society and less frequently exhorts the Councils to forgive him. Instead, he writes with newfound fervor for his scientific exploration. This shift signifies his increasing independence from the society around him because it shows him finding truth in the external world rather than in the opinions of others. Nevertheless, at this point in the novella, Equality 7-2521 still worries about the conventions of society, especially about the fact that his discoveries are his alone. Later, he breaks entirely with such conventions, but here he still doubts what he thinks he knows about himself and the world around him. Such doubts allow us to witness the slow and gradual process of his leaving society.

The content of the conversations that Equality 7-2521 has with others constitutes important markers of his progress toward an eventual break from his society. Because these conversations are rare—*Anthem* consists almost entirely of musings about the state of the natural and human world and thus often bears resemblance to a scientific journal or a religious meditation—they gain even greater significance in their function as expressions of individual will. Equality 7-2521's conversation with International 4-8818 in Chapter I demonstrates Equality 7-2521's willingness to break the law in pursuit of truth. His conversation with the Golden One here builds upon his growing desire for freedom from the society that constrains him. His calling her "dearest one," which evidences his increasing attraction to her, demonstrates his willingness to break the law in the pursuit of love.

The conversation between the Golden One and Equality 7-2521 is rife with biblical imagery, both in their naming of each other and her giving him water to cool him. Naming, the original power of man in Genesis, makes the Golden One and Equality 7-2521 more intimate with each other and establishes their possession of each other. Interestingly, though Liberty 5-3000 is referred to throughout *Anthem* as "the Golden One," the name Equality 7-2521 assigns to her, her name for him does not appear again in the text. Feminists argue that this disparity marks the fundamental inequality in Rand's view of men and women, though Rand might say that the issue is entirely stylistic: after all, Equality 7-2521 is writing the text, and it would be hard to incorporate the Golden One's name for him into the text in a meaningful way.

The offering of water is important both because it represents the Golden One's assumption of the role of caretaker and also because it is laden with biblical imagery. In offering water to Equality 7-2521, the Golden One adopts a role as caretaker and comfortgiver—a role feminists might argue Rand prescribes for her out of a heightened sense of the traditional roles of women. The offering of water is significant also, however, because it is an image very common in the Judeo-Christian Bible. According to the New Testament, Jesus Christ often asked and received water from townspeople he met in his travels, and the sharing of water is considered to be a virtue, as it represents the giving of life-sustaining respite from the heat and weariness of travel. Notably, Christ usually made followers of those who gave him water to drink. In this case, the Golden One's giving water to Equality 7-2521 accompanies her conversion into obedience of him, represents her comforting of him, and is also shot through with sexual overtones. As she nurtures Equality 7-2521, he desires her and she desires him shamelessly for the first time in the novella. Rand seems to be conjoining the conversion experience and the sexual experience into one baffling moment of ecstasy.

CHAPTERS V–VI

SUMMARY: CHAPTER V

Equality 7-2521 discovers how to make a lightbulb work. He believes he alone has made light. He has found the materials for making the lightbulb in the tunnel where he is hiding, and he has used wires to make electricity flow through the lightbulb and produce light. He is amazed that the light has come from the heart of the metal, without flint or fire. He compares the glowing flint to the crack in the walls of a prison. Equality 7-2521 realizes the meaning of the lightbulb—that he can provide clean and bright light for all the cities in the world—and he determines that his discovery is too important not to be shared with the world. He concludes that electricity is the key to harnessing nature's power and that he must bring it to the world.

Equality 7-2521 also concludes that he must be allowed into the Home of the Scholars, where there are rooms to experiment and where he can ask the help of the other scholars, in whom he has great faith. He concludes that there is enough work ahead that all the scholars of the world should work together to make progress with his new invention.

A month later, the World Council of Scholars, a group of the wisest scholars from all over the world, is to convene for its annual meeting, and this year, the meeting is in Equality 7-2521's city. He resolves to go to the World Council and show them his invention. He will tell the council members the whole story of its discovery, and he believes they will be so impressed that they will forgive him for all his sins and transgressions. He decides that the World Council will speak to the Council of Vocations and have him reassigned from street sweeper to scholar so that he may continue his research.

Equality 7-2521 resolves to guard his tunnel with his life because no one but the World Council of Scholars will understand the significance of the light, and the light is the most important thing. In mid-thought, he suddenly realizes that he cares about his body. He believes the lightbulb is a part of his physical being and he wants to see the body that helped bring the bulb into existence. Until this point, he has never seen his body, but now he stretches out his arms and legs and realizes his own strength. Despite knowing that it is wrong to want it, he wants to see his own reflection.

SUMMARY: CHAPTER VI

Equality 7-2521 writes that he was so excited about his discovery of the lightbulb that he forgot to pay attention to the time, and he was late in returning to the Home of the Street Sweepers. The Council of the Home asked him where he was, and he would not answer. Without emotion, the Council ordered Equality 7-2521 to be held in the Palace of Corrective Detention until he told the Council where he had been.

Equality 7-2521 writes that at the Palace of Correction, he was stripped and tied to a post where he was whipped and beaten while being asked where he had been. He lost consciousness and woke in a cell, happy that he had not betrayed the tunnel and the light. He stayed in the cell in the Palace of Corrective Detention until he realized that it was the day before the meeting of the World Council of Scholars. He then broke out of the Palace, which was easy because no precautions had been taken to prevent escape since no one had ever tried to do so before. He snuck back to his tunnel, where he writes this entry, reveling in the idea that the next day will bring atonement and reunification with his brothers.

ANALYSIS: CHAPTERS V–VI

Equality 7-2521's belief that the lightbulb is too significant not to be shared, a belief that comes to have disastrous consequences for him, represents exactly the kind of thinking against which Rand is writing. He thinks that the lightbulb, a technological innovation, can be the crack in the wall of his prison, a way to reach all the members of his society and share with them what he has discovered in his tunnel. Rand shows, through Equality 7-2521, how such thinking leads to painful results. She believes that invention and progress are worthy not because they help the masses but rather in and of themselves, because they are the result of the individual mind working and expressing itself.

This section is the most hopeful part of the novella, and it is in this section that we most identify with Equality 7-2521. Here, he still wants to make the world a better place for himself and for his brothers, and he believes he has a way to do so. Moreover, the harsh punishment visited on Equality 7-2521 when he returns late from the tunnel and will not tell the Council where he has been foreshadows the violence that we fear will be brought to bear against him at the World Council. Though Rand claims not to have imbued *Anthem* with a traditional structure, this section, in which we sympathize with Equality 7-2521, builds the story's tension and gives us the expectation of a climax in the coming confrontation with the World Council of Scholars.

Equality 7-2521's sense of self-worth is entirely caught up in the significance of the lightbulb, as is the proper result, in Rand's view, of allowing for individual benefit from individual discovery. Equality 7-2521's increasing vanity and his desire to know his own strength are related to his belief that he has discovered something important and that his body is worth knowing. Thus, even after he has been beaten, he revels in his own strength at not succumbing to the beating and revealing his tunnel and the lightbulb. He harnesses his own strength at the same time he harnesses the strength of electricity, and he takes equal pride in both. His willingness to suffer for the lightbulb stems from his belief that the invention is an extension of his own physical being and is more important than his own body, which he has only recently begun to value.

The scene in the Palace of Corrective Detention in which Equality 7-2521 is flogged while bound naked to a post directly correlates to the Christian story about the scourging of Christ at the pillar. In the Christian story, Christ is dragged before the Roman authorities, stripped of his clothes, and beaten mercilessly at a pillar while being mocked by Roman soldiers shortly before being crucified. Rand uses the scene here to heighten our sense that Equality 7-2521 is a new prophet who must suffer great abuses, at the hands of tormenters, in the interest of his beliefs. By comparing Equality 7-2521 to Christ, Rand may offend some readers who believe that Christ is the son of God and that such comparisons are irreverent, and she may well have intended to give offense. She often said she was trying to reclaim religious language from religion, in order to prove that it was possible to worship an ideal without believing in the supernatural. The blatant comparison that this scene at the post invites is an attempt to reclaim religious imagery as well, just as is the heavy-handed image of Equality 7-2521 as the bringer of light to the world.

This section, like others in the novella, contains countless contrasting pairs, which emphasize, often blatantly, the battle between shapeless, nameless evil and vain, proud good. Specifically, Equality 7-2521's high emotion and proud intentions contrast directly with the Council's boredom while sentencing him to the Palace of Corrective Detention. The violence of the Council also contrasts with Equality 7-2521's passive resistance. Similarly, the light of the bulb, weak though it is, significantly outshines the darkness of a society lit only by candles. Furthermore, Equality 7-2521's care in protecting his tunnel stands in opposition to the carelessness of those in charge of guarding the Palace of Corrective Detention. These pairings further highlight Rand's belief that everything about Equality 7-2521 makes different from those around him. Society wallows in apathetic, dim insecurity, while Equality 7-2521 covetously guards his precious light. In these pairings, society always comprises the weaker half, with much less invested, while Equality 7-2521, fighting bitterly and to the death for his ideals, always comprises the stronger half.

CHAPTER VII

"Many men in the Homes of the Scholars have had strange new ideas in the past . . . but when the majority of their brother Scholars voted against them, they abandoned their ideas, as all men must."

(See QUOTATIONS, p. 50)

SUMMARY

Equality 7-2521 writes from the forest to which he has fled that he has abandoned hope and believes he will sleep on the grass for a few days until the beasts come to eat his body. He feels that he has aged a lifetime in this day. He recounts the events of the day: he is able to walk right into the meeting of the World Council of Scholars because there are no guards to stop him. The first thing he notices is the sky shining in the windows and a painting on the wall, depicting the twenty men who invented the candle. The shapeless forms of the scholars are huddled around a long table. As he enters, the scholars turn to him, but they do not know what to think. He addresses them in a loud voice and in greeting.

Collective 0-0009, the oldest and wisest of the scholars, asks Equality 7-2521 who he is, and Equality 7-2521 gives him his name and tells him he is a street sweeper. The scholars are angry and scared that a street sweeper should have interrupted their meeting. Equality 7-2521 stops their murmurs by telling them he has brought them the greatest gift ever presented to mankind, and they listen to him while he tells them the story of the invention of the lightbulb, the tunnel, and his incarceration in the Palace of Corrective Detention. The scholars hear out his story, but when he lights the lightbulb, they become terrified and huddle against the walls, trembling together. Equality 7-2521 laughs at them and tells them that he has tamed the sky for them and has presented to them the key of the earth.

Collective 0-0009 lambasts Equality 7-2521 for breaking all the laws of their society and even boasting of doing so. The other scholars begin slinging insults and threats at Equality 7-2521, telling him they will have him burned at the stake or lashed to death. Equality 7-2521 tells them he does not care what they do with his body but that he wants them only to protect the light. The scholars tell him that what is not achieved collectively cannot be good and what is not thought by all men cannot be true. They tell him that there have often been scholars who thought they had brilliants ideas, but when their brothers voted against them, they abandoned their work. They worry that the light will ruin the Department of Candles, which was only recently established and took great labor to be ratified, and that it will ruin the plans of the World Council, without which not even the sun can rise. One scholar concludes that if the light lightens the toil of men, it is evil because toil is the end for which men exist. The scholars conclude that the light will be destroyed.

Equality 7-2521 cannot abide the destruction of the lightbulb, so he grabs his invention and flees the council. He runs blindly until he collapses and discovers he is in the Uncharted Forest, where he supposes he will die alone. He realizes, however, that he had been lying to himself, that he did not create the light for his brothers but rather for its own sake. He does not regret building the light and pursuing his scientific discoveries, though he wishes he could see the Golden One again.

> *"[I]f this should lighten the toil of men . . . then it is a great evil, for men have no cause to exist save in toiling for other men."*   (See QUOTATIONS, p. 51)

ANALYSIS

In Collective 0-0009, Rand exposes the mastermind behind the demise of the old world. Until we meet Collective 0-0009, we might suppose that the failings of Equality 7-2521's society are grounded in the failings of individuals who do not realize their potential or are stupid, weak, and helpless. Rand's view of the collectivist society, however, holds that it systematically rejects progress and perpetuates hurtful cycles of working for others. Thus the failure of technology stems not from the failure of scientists to develop technologies or the failure of the average citizen to take advantage of those technologies, but rather the failure of the World Council of Scholars to come to a consensus about how to utilize the new technologies. Additionally, the Council is afraid of the lightbulb, even though Equality 7-2521 promises to harness its power for them. Their ingrained fear of new things becomes public policy and makes a system of the repression of progress.

This distinction—that society at large rather than certain individuals are holding humankind back—is very important to the political criticism that *Anthem* makes. Rand is arguing against a position that holds that socialism and collectivism are fundamentally useful and good propositions but were simply executed poorly in Russia. This position holds that Communism in Russia was a failure in large part because of the corruption, vanity, and cruelty of men like Josef Stalin, who lined their own pockets and carried out personal vendettas rather than truly pursue the good of the people. Rand, on the other hand, believes that collectivism is evil and doomed to fail no matter how it is executed, and the individual who fights for his own well-being over that of his brothers is the only effective solution to the problems inherent in collectivism.

Equality 7-2521's conflict with the World Council of Scholars forms the central event of *Anthem* and comes closest to being the climax of the story, because it is the point at which there is no turning back for Equality 7-2521. His smaller transgressions—preferring International 4-8818, falling in love with the Golden One and speaking to her as a lover, seeking the solitude of the tunnel, and creating the lightbulb—could potentially be forgiven and have not cut Equality 7-2521 off irreparably from his society. Once the World Council rejects the lightbulb, however, all hope of reconciliation vanishes, and Equality 7-2521's path clears. Even though Equality 7-2521 himself does not see the path before him, it is inevitable that he break with society and seek his own way in the Uncharted Forest.

Rand claims that *Anthem* does not have traditional structure and that it does not have a meaningful plot. For her, the novella revolves entirely around the internal conflict inside Equality 7-2521's mind. This conflict resolves itself in the final chapters of the novella and provides the jumping-off point for the most philosophical part of the story, the actual anthem of the title. Here, however, despite Rand's claims about the novella's lack of formal structure, it is possible to identify a likely candidate for the climax of the story. The conflict with the World Council becomes inevitable in this chapter, and this conflict, and the resulting exile of Equality 7-2521, helps cause Equality 7-2521's crucial realization that he is an individual and that his individuality is more important than his place in society.

Equality 7-2521's realization that he actually created light for his own good and for its own sake conflicts with his earlier belief that he should present the lightbulb for the good of his brothers. Rand wants us to see this changed point of view as a kind of self-actualization. She believes that Equality 7-2521 has been deluding himself about his motivations and that he can realize his true feelings only now that he is free of social constraints and returned to a state of nature. This contention is troublesome, however, for it threatens the infallibility of the individual, whom Rand cherishes so much. Her statement that Equality 7-2521 has always known the truth but has not realized this truth is tantamount to second-guessing him, which is in tension with her belief that what the individual thinks and believes is sacred and should be followed at all costs.

CHAPTER VIII

SUMMARY

Equality 7-2521 wakes in the forest and realizes that for the first time in his life, he is waking because he is rested and not because someone is ringing a bell to wake him. He observes the forest in some detail, and it seems magnificent to him. He stretches his body out on the moss, and he laughs and laughs for no reason except that he is free. He realizes that he can stay asleep and lie on the moss as long as he wants. His body, of its own volition, jumps up and whirls around in a circle.

Equality 7-2521 takes his lightbulb and heads into the forest. The forest is dense, and as he works through the leaves, he compares the forest to the sea, thinking of the bushes as waves below him, spraying up into the treetops. When he is hungry, Equality 7-2521 stops and uses a single stone as an arrow to kill a bird. He cooks the bird and eats it. He finds great satisfaction in killing the bird and is surprised to find that he takes pride in eating.

Equality 7-2521 then comes to a stream, where he stops to drink. He sees his reflection for the first time, and it takes his breath away. He is frozen in front of the stream staring at his own image. He discovers he does not look like his brothers, because they are shapeless, formless, and downtrodden while he is thin, strong, and lithe. He is hard and strong and concludes that he can trust himself and has nothing to fear of his own company.

Equality 7-2521 has walked through the forest all day when he suddenly remembers that he is exiled from society, or, in his words, "Damned." He laughs because he does not care that he is damned. It is the only time he thinks of what he has left behind. Equality 7-2521 tells us that he is writing on the same paper he used in the tunnel. He intends to write a great deal because he concludes he has a great deal to say to himself. At the moment, however, there is too much he does not understand to continue writing.

ANALYSIS

Equality 7-2521's return to nature to escape the evils of man reflects Rand's belief that only other men can limit the freedom of a man and that in the state of nature man is completely free. This theme is common in philosophy, especially in the work of eighteenth-century Swiss philosopher Jean-Jacques Rousseau who, in his *Confessions,* suggests that man was a superior being before society and its constructs weakened his constitution. In *Anthem,* in the forest, where he has been forbidden by society to go, Equality 7-2521 experiences the joy of his body for the first time when he is not oppressed by work assigned to him by others and the yoke of collectivism. His legs return him to the state of nature instinctively because, for Rand, individualism constitutes a near-instinct, a feeling so ingrained in human make-up that it cannot be completely abolished and will be rediscovered, as Equality 7-2521 has rediscovered it, under even the most dire circumstances.

For Rand, physical beauty and athletic prowess accompany intellectual and moral perfection naturally, and the two combine in Equality 7-2521 to create what she considers an ideal man. Vanity and pride are both positive attributes in Rand's thinking, which is why she relates the story of Equality 7-2521's discovery of his own reflection with no irony. The incident closely resembles the story of Narcissus, the Greek mythological character who became so obsessed with his own reflection that he sat at the edge of a pool staring at it until he became a flower. Nevertheless, in *Anthem,* Equality 7-2521's self-admiration is a form of self-discovery and liberation from social convention. Additionally, the episode of Equality 7-2521 feeding himself is a manifestation of his perfection. Though as a street sweeper Equality 7-2521 has never been hunting for birds before and has probably never cooked a bird before, he fells a bird with a single throw of a sharp rock, cooks the bird over a fire, and very much enjoys his meal because he is a perfect man, capable of succeeding in everything he tries, even when it is completely new to him. Rand often referred to herself as a Romantic, by which she meant that she was concerned chiefly with the ideal. Omitting details such as Equality 7-2521's probable first ten tries to kill the bird is an example of her disregard for realistic detail in favor of imbuing her heroes with perfection befitting her ideal.

Equality 7-2521's return to nature also signals Rand's presentation of Equality 7-2521 as the new Adam, the creator of the true human race. Here, he is at one with nature and at peace with his body, and he has returned to Eden. In the biblical story of Genesis, Adam and Eve live in harmony in the Garden of Eden until a serpent tempts Eve with fruit from the tree of knowledge. When they eat the fruit, Adam and Eve become aware of their own bodies and selves. When God, who has forbidden them to eat of the tree of knowledge, discovers their sin, he throws them out of the garden and into the world, where they spawn a flawed race of men. The parallel is turned on its head here, however, by Equality 7-2521's realization that he is, in fact, an outcast. For Rand, Eden is a place that can be re-entered by using knowledge itself. Ironically, it takes becoming an outcast for Equality 7-2521 to realize where he will be able to find happiness and self-awareness. For Rand, self-awareness is saving, not damning.

Technology and nature, often in tension in literature, are means to the same end in *Anthem*. Nature provides man a chance to prove himself, a way to make it on his own. It belongs to him because he is a man, and the natural order is such that the forest welcomes him into its keep. Technology, likewise, belongs to man because he has created it. He creates it because it is progress and it exalts him. Interestingly, the emphasis on nature in *Anthem* is not present in Rand's other works, where the emphasis is chiefly on the city and man's achievements. In *Anthem*, however, Rand emphasizes that man is the master of all creation, and that he can use his mind to master even those elements, such as lightning and electricity, that seem to master him. Indeed, Rand often suggests that the world is meaningless without man's mind in it to give it meaning, and in this way, technology is the complement of nature because technology is essentially a natural force with the direction of man's will behind it.

CHAPTER IX

Several days later, Equality 7-2521 begins writing in his journal for the first time since he entered the Uncharted Forest. As he is walking through the forest, Equality 7-2521 hears footsteps behind him and discovers that the Golden One has followed him into the forest. He asks her how she came to be in the forest, and she answers, swaying with her fists at her side, only that she has found him. He asks her again, and she tells him that she has followed him because she heard talk all over the city of his encounter with the World Council of Scholars and his fleeing into the Uncharted Forest.

The Golden One is tattered from the journey through the forest, but she is not weary or afraid. She tells Equality 7-2521 she wants to share in his damnation and to follow him wherever he goes. Her voice is bitter and triumphant as she tells him that he is harder, prouder, and more beautiful than her brothers. She begs him to do what he will with her but not to send her away, and she bows in front of him. He raises her to her feet and kisses her, amazed by the very idea of kissing. They stand together for a long time.

Equality 7-2521 tells the Golden One that there is nothing to fear in the forest or in their solitude, and he suggests that they forget their brothers and remember only that they are together and have joy between them. He declares the world their own, and they walk through the forest hand in hand. That night they have sex, and Equality 7-2521 realizes that sex is the only ecstasy in a man's life.

Equality 7-2521 and the Golden One walk for several days together and make bows and arrows to kill birds. At night, they sleep in a ring of campfires, to keep out the beasts. They plan to stop and build a house some day, and they see their days together as endless. When Equality 7-2521 begins to be puzzled by his new life, he hurries ahead and forgets his troubles as he watches the Golden One following him. She is completely obedient to him and does not question him about anything.

For the first time in his life, Equality 7-2521 begins to doubt the laws he was taught by the society in which he lived. He questions how it can be that everything that is solitude is evil when he and the Golden One are pursuing solitude in such happiness. He observes that the only things that have ever given him joy in his life are the lightbulb and the Golden One, neither of which has anything to do with his brothers. He concludes that both these joys come from himself alone. He also begins to suspect that there is some error in the way he has been thinking up to this point, that there is some word that is missing from his vocabulary, but he does not know what it is.

The Golden One tries to tell Equality 7-2521 that she loves him, but she does not know how to say the word "I." She tells him that "[w]e love you," but she is not satisfied with this articulation of her feelings, and she gropes for something more personal but does not know how to express it. The moment leaves both of them feeling confused.

ANALYSIS

Feminists are troubled by Rand's view of women, especially by the Golden One's subservience to Equality 7-2521 and her inherent inability to create solutions to her intellectual puzzles without the help of Equality 7-2521. They note that the Golden One is never appreciated for her own worth but instead is worshipped as an object, that even her name is somewhat insulting in that it characterizes her by the color of her hair, and that she has virtually no part in the story except as the thing that Equality 7-2521 adores. Rand might answer that when the Golden One bows in front of Equality 7-2521, she is merely acknowledging the perfection in him and offering him herself as equally perfect. After all, she would say, Equality 7-2521 is drawn to her as much as she is drawn to him, and her fleeing society to chase him into the forest represents as great a break with society as his confrontation with the World Council of Scholars. Moreover, Rand might say, the Golden One suspects at the same time that Equality 7-2521 does that the lack of the word "I" is a major problem. Nevertheless, feminists are not satisfied with the continuous emphasis on the Golden One's dependence on Equality 7-2521 and her constantly following him while he offers her no reciprocal form of trust. They argue that Equality 7-2521's observation that the lightbulb and the Golden One both spring from himself belittles the Golden One, who is, after all, not the actual invention of Equality 7-2521. Rand might respond that she is merely mimicking the biblical story of Adam and Eve, in which Eve springs from Adam's rib and is, in a certain sense, an extension of her husband.

Rand presents several ways of testing the world around us in *Anthem,* and ultimately she concludes that the best way to make determinations about the world is to test them against our own inner reactions. As Equality 7-2521 begins to doubt his society for the first time, he engages in a kind of thought process previously foreign to him in that he begins to compare what he is discovering of the world to what he has been taught of it. Notably, the way that Equality 7-2521 uncovers truths about the world is very different from the way he proceeds earlier with his scientific experiments. In his experiments, he proceeds like a good scientist, tinkering and tooling until his lightbulb works, and testing and retesting, while isolating factors, to discover electricity. When investigating facts about the world, however, Equality 7-2521 proceeds largely by instinct, so that he is called by his heart to discover that there is some word missing from his vocabulary, but he does not have an experiment to perform to determine what it is. Likewise, when he is trying to discover what makes him happy, he proceeds chiefly through induction, observing which things make him happy and determining where those things come from, in order to determine how happiness comes to be. To determine what is true about human nature, he must act as his own instrument.

Anthem's extensive foreshadowing gives away many of the secrets of the story before Rand reveals them. The Golden One's attempt to say "I love you," for example, is one of several events that foreshadow the massive revelation, at the end of *Anthem,* that the individual is the center of the universe. The Transgressor of the Unspeakable Word's death in Chapter II, before which he specifically seeks out Equality 7-2521 as he burns in the town square, also presages the coming realization that what Equality 7-2521 has been missing is the word "I." Most obvious, the language of the entire novella, which uses the first person plural "we" to refer to the individual is a major clue that the resolution of the story's conflict involves a shift in the language. Indeed, taken as a whole, these clues leave very little suspense in *Anthem*. It is fairly clear from the outset and at every step of the way that Rand is leading us to an ego-centered world. The lack of suspense, however, which reinforces the idea that *Anthem* is more political manifesto than fiction, allows Rand to drive her point home time and again without making us wonder where she is headed.

CHAPTERS X–XI

SUMMARY: CHAPTER X

Equality 7-2521 and the Golden One climb up into the mountains so that no one can follow them. They have hiked for several days when they see what they believe to be a fire but in actuality is the sun reflecting off the windows of an abandoned house. It is a two-story house with huge windows. Equality 7-2521 wonders how the house remains standing with so little wall to hold it up. They determine that it must be a house from the Unmentionable Times that was protected from the weather and time by trees. Equality 7-2521 asks the Golden One whether she is afraid, but she tells him she is not.

Equality 7-2521 and the Golden One enter the house, and they are amazed at the house and its technology. They are astounded by the idea that a house could be so small, such that it obviously housed no more than a dozen people. They are amazed by the colors in the house, as well, and are shocked to learn that houses could be a color other than white, brown, or gray. They discover mirrors and light-bulbs. They then find the bedroom and discover that it contains only two beds and they conclude that only two people lived there, and they are amazed by the privacy.

In the closet, Equality 7-2521 and the Golden One find clothes, and the Golden One is amazed at the sight of so many colors. Many of the clothes have turned to dust, but many survive. Equality 7-2521 also finds a library with shelves of books, and he is amazed that there are not manuscripts. He looks through some of the books and discovers that he knows the language but that there are many words he does not know. Equality 7-2521 tells the Golden One that they will move into the house and never leave it. They will not share it but will live there together until they die. The Golden One answers, "Your will be done."

Equality 7-2521 goes out into the forest around the house, gathers wood and water, and kills a mountain goat to cook for dinner. The Golden One does not help him because she cannot be torn away from the mirror, where she stands staring at her own body. After sunset, the Golden One falls asleep in front of the mirror amid the finery she has discovered in the house, and Equality 7-2521 carries her to bed. He then lights a candle and returns to the library to read through the night, too excited to sleep.

As he stares out on the night below him and the sky above, he meditates on his new commandment to live and speak and give meaning to the world. He seeks guidance in his heart, and stares at his hands where he sees the history of centuries, both good and evil, and he is filled with reverence and pity. He wonders what the secret is that his heart is begging to tell him.

Summary: Chapter XI

"I am. I think. I will."

(See QUOTATIONS, p. 52)

Equality 7-2521 realizes the meaning of the word "I" and realizes what has been missing from his world. He writes about standing at the summit of a mountain and concludes that he has reached the end of his quest to find the meaning of things because he is the meaning of things. His eyes' seeing makes the earth beautiful, and his ears' hearing makes the earth sing. His mind's searching gives the earth

SUMMARY & ANALYSIS

truth. His will is the only command he respects or should respect. In his new view, the only three holy words are "I will it!"

Equality 7-2521 realizes that the goal of his existence, no matter what may come of the earth, is his personal happiness. He is not a means to an end, and he is not a servant of his brothers. His miracles are his and his alone, and he will protect them from others at all costs. He says that his treasures are his thoughts, his will, and his freedom, and the greatest of these is freedom. He owes nothing to his brothers. They owe him nothing, and he wants nothing from them. Those of his brothers who earn his honor will have it, but they will not have it just by virtue of being fellow men. He chooses his friends and he chooses when to join with them and when not to. He neither commands nor obeys.

In Equality 7-2521's newfound view, the word "we" must always be a second thought to men, after the word "I." When it is allowed to become a primary thought, it is the root of all evil and becomes a great lie. The word "we" enables the weak to steal from the strong and becomes a stone that crushes all those beneath it. Equality 7-2521 vows that he is finished with the old society and collectivism. He has seen the face of god, and he will raise it above the earth so that everyone may worship at its altar. His new god is "I."

ANALYSIS: CHAPTERS X–XI

Equality 7-2521's switch from the use of the word "we" to the use of the word "I" to mean himself signals the internal resolution of *Anthem*. Chapter XI is the culmination of all that Equality 7-2521 has learned about the evils of collectivism is the first time he sees clearly. In the sense that the novella is really about a man's internal battle with himself to discover individualism, Chapter XI could be considered the resolution of the story's conflict. Rand herself considered Chapters XI and XII to be the most important in the story. They are the place where she lays out in plain language the meaning of objectivism, egoism, and individualism. These philosophies place the individual above all else, and they savor freedom over the goods of society. Rand suggests that society should be sought out only when a person chooses it, as a second thought to what the individual wants, and that it should be only with those people whom the individual chooses. In Rand's view, any other kind of life, in which another person is more important than or as important as the self, is a lie that ultimately brings about great evil.

Critics of Rand are repulsed by the blatant selfishness she professes. They argue that humankind comes together into society in order to provide and be provided for, and that in the company of others, humans gain as much from their peers as they give to them. Religious critics and others also argue that the individual has a moral obligation to care for those less fortunate than him- or herself. Rand directly engages these critics by mocking well-known passages of the New Testament. In his letter to the Corinthians, St. Paul writes that the three things that endure are faith, hope, and love, and the greatest of these is love. He says that love endures beyond even the end of the world, when faith and hope are no longer necessary virtues. Rand is deliberately offering a different triptych with her lofty estimation of thought, will, and freedom. She suggests, by implication, that of these, freedom is the cornerstone of all life and that without it nothing else endures. Moreover, Rand often announced that she was writing directly against those who believed that selfishness was a vice. She was offering an entirely new way of living, and she believed that it was the only way to live.

The language and imagery of *Anthem,* in addition to being laden with religious and philosophic references, is extraordinarily heavy-handed. In his moment of triumph, Equality 7-2521 stands on a mountain top at dawn—quite a melodramatic image. In his lowest moments, he suffers at the hands of men less worthy than he in a dungeon at the Palace of Corrective Detention. In this way, Rand offers a philosophy that is very easy to navigate. When she wants to mark a character as good, she makes him or her beautiful and strong. When she wants to mark a character as evil, on the other hand, she makes him or her ugly and weak. The most obvious example of this dichotomy comes in the form of the Golden One, whose physical beauty is unsurpassed, and who is, as her name suggests, blonde. By contrast, the council members are shapeless and frightened. This same kind of opposition appears in the explanation of Rand's philosophy: collectivism is like stone, crushing those beneath it, while freedom is a treasure, and the sense of self is a god to be exalted and worshipped. Rand wants us to read *Anthem* seriously, in a straightforward manner. The imagery is meant to guide us directly to the right answer, the right philosophy, with a minimum of guessing and side-tracking.

CHAPTER XII

But I still wonder how it was possible, in those
graceless years of transition, long ago, that men did
not see whither they were going, and went on, in
blindness and cowardice, to their fate.

(See QUOTATIONS, p. 53)

SUMMARY

Equality 7-2521 tells us that he has discovered the word "I" while
reading the books in his library. The discovery moves him to tremendous elation and pity for mankind. After he has read for some
time, he calls the Golden One to him and tells her about what he has
found. She listens and then tells him she loves him. He then decides
that they each need a new name. He names himself Prometheus, and
he names her Gaea. She accepts her name without comment.

Equality 7-2521 concludes that the Transgressor of the Unspeakable Word, whom he saw burned at the stake in his youth, chose him
as his heir to carry on his crusade after he was gone. He resolves to
live in his new home and kill and raise his own food and learn the
secrets of the Unmentionable Times from the books in the house. He
will rebuild the world that has disintegrated at the hands of the collectivists because he is not shackled to the weakest of his society. He
will build a fence of wires around his house so that no one from his
old city can come onto his property unless he chooses to allow them.

The Golden One becomes pregnant, and Equality 7-2521
resolves that his son will be raised as a real man who takes pride in
his own existence. He will work to get his house into working order
and his land planted, and when he has succeeded in renovating and
restoring his home, he will go back to the city and gather the few
people, including his friend International 4-8818, whose spirits
have not been broken by society. He will bring them up to his home
to begin a new race.

Equality 7-2521 meditates on human history. He says that man
was first enslaved by the gods, but that he broke free from the gods.
Man was then enslaved by kings, but he revolted from the kings. He
was then enslaved by his birth, kin, and race, and he broke free from
all these things. He declared himself to have naturally endowed
rights of which he could not be deprived.

Equality 7-2521 wonders about everything that men have lost in
the name of collectivism and why men could not see their demise

coming. He concludes that there must have been some men who did see it coming and suffered great agonies during the fall, and he wishes he had a way to tell them across time that their hope is not forever lost. He concludes that man's spirit will always prevail over the evils of collectivism, though it may take time. He resolves that he will bring back the lost world for the sake of man's freedom, rights, life, and honor. Even if his new race fails, its members' sense of individualism will never die because these members are united under the most important word in human history: "ego."

ANALYSIS

The renaming of the Golden One and Equality 7-2521 signals their complete transformation from the social creatures they are early on in *Anthem* into the free individuals they now are. Prometheus, the name Equality 7-2521 chooses for himself, was a Greek man who crept up to Olympus, the home of the gods, and stole fire from them. He brought the fire back down to humans, enabling them to cook and have light at nighttime. Equality 7-2521 chooses the name Prometheus for himself in part as a reference to his inventing the lightbulb and in part because he believes he will bring a new philosophy of individualism to the earth. Gaea, whose name Equality 7-2521 gives to the Golden One, was the Greek mother earth, who gave birth to the other gods and goddesses as well as to the sky and the sea. He chooses this name for her because she will, in his belief, give birth to a race of gods to rule the earth. Feminists object to the naming of the Golden One, who has now been named twice by her mate, and who apparently has no independent sense of self-worth. Moreover, the name Gaea promotes her as the mother of the new race but essentially makes of her nothing more than a vessel for Equality 7-2521's offspring. Rand might argue, however, that the Golden One is an active participant in the new world and that her part is to make the world beautiful and to endow her children with a sense of individualism. The characters' assumption of new names signifies that their break with society, which begins with the presentation of the lightbulb to the World Council of Scholars, is now complete and final.

Critics of Rand's philosophy take issue with Equality 7-2521's winner-takes-all attitude and apparent dreams of world domination. They take issue with the fact that he co-opts the home in the forest without knowing to whom it belongs and then immediately

cordons it off as his own. Furthermore, they say, Rand's champion-
ing of a new race of man has particularly sinister connotations given
that *Anthem* was published in the United States on the heels of Nazi
leader Adolf Hitler's defeat during World War II. Given that Hitler
too advocated the founding of a superior race of men, specifically by
killing off those he believed were weighing society down, *Anthem*'s
appearance was particularly ill-timed. Rand's advocates, however,
would point out that she is declaring the supremacy of human rights
and that she believes each man is endowed with them. They would
argue further that Rand stands in direct opposition to the kind of
authoritarian oppression manifest in Hitler's Nazi regime because it
deprives men of the chance to participate in the world as human
beings with natural rights and a sense of their own worth. No one,
they would say, should be deprived of his or her rights or life in the
name of the collective society.

Rand sends a message to her contemporaries fighting for individualism with Equality 7-2521's remarks that he wishes he could
carry a message to those past generations that suffered during the
transition period. Since Rand sees her own time as the transition
from the glory of individualism, represented by the United States in
the 1890s and 1920s, to the age of collectivism, represented by Russia starting around 1917, she wants both to warn those who believe
in collectivism about its dangers and to bolster those who are still
holding up the resistance in the name of the individual. For this reason, her hero speaks directly to those crusaders for the ego and tells
them that no matter how bleak things may look, the individual will
survive, and with him, the possibility of rebirth. The political nature
of *Anthem* comes through most clearly in this last section too in
which Rand lays out her plan to bring back the individual and
encourages those who are helping her do so. In this way, she herself
is acting as a sort of political prophet, ushering in the new age that
she describes through Equality 7-2521's vision, and this prophesy-
ing proves the driving force of the whole novella.

Important Quotations Explained

1. There was no pain in their eyes and no knowledge of the agony of their body. There was only joy in them, and pride, a pride holier than it is fit for human pride to be.

While he watches the Transgressor of the Unspeakable Word burn at the stake in Chapter II, Equality 7-2521 makes this observation about the Transgressor's stoicism. The word the Transgressor has spoken is "I," a concept forbidden in the society because everyone must work for the good of his or her brothers and any thought that occurs in private is necessarily evil. The Transgressor does not believe in collectivism, and he finds Equality 7-2521 in the crowd and locks eyes with him while he dies, a moment that Equality 7-2521 concludes marks him and destines him to start a new race of men who are individuals. It is the same kind of stoicism that Equality 7-2521 himself demonstrates when he is incarcerated and beaten at the Palace of Corrective Detention for refusing to tell the council about his tunnel when he returns late to the Home of the Street Sweepers.

Equality 7-2521's observation about the peaceful and even euphoric nature of the Transgressor of the Unspoken Word's death relates closely to Rand's belief that humans do not feel bodily pain when they suffer for the sake of an ideal. Rand's heroes do not feel fear or remorse about their social sins when they are committed in the name of a higher good, namely, the individual. Indeed, for Rand, any action grounded in the individual's sense of self is admirable. The Transgressor is the only character in *Anthem*, other than Equality 7-2521 and the Golden One, who demonstrates a sense of self-worth and a willingness to suffer for his autonomy and who thus rises above the constraints of his society.

2.   "Many men in the Homes of the Scholars have had
     strange new ideas in the past . . . but when the
     majority of their brother Scholars voted against them,
     they abandoned their ideas, as all men must."

These words of a member of the World Council of Scholars, which
exiles Equality 7-2521 after he presents his lightbulb, in
Chapter VII, reflect the view, pervasive in Equality 7-2521's society,
that any idea not held by all men is worthless. Equality 7-2521's
confidence in the usefulness of his invention is irrelevant, as the
council cares not about advancing scientific progress but rather
about controlling it. The World Council will not act unless all its
members agree and, as a result, has not approved any technological
progress in the last hundred years. The philosophy expounded here
by the council member reflects the ideals of collectivism, against
which the whole of *Anthem* is written. Rand believes that when
society acts based on consensus, the weakest members of society
drag down the most exemplary members, with the result that society never achieves its maximum potential. This system represents
the *we* that Rand considers the ultimate evil in society and against
which all her heroes, including Equality 7-2521, fight.

3.   "[I]f this should lighten the toil of men . . . then it is a
      great evil, for men have no cause to exist save in
      toiling for other men."

This opinion, which a member of the World Council of Scholars
voices in Chapter VII, reflects one of the crucial tenets of collectivism. Not only must all decisions be made by committee, but all men
must work not for their own profit but for the benefit of their brothers. If men's lives are really aimed only at toil, then all pleasure,
progress, and invention are barred to them, according to Rand, who
believes that the kind of thinking exhibited by the World Council of
Scholars leads to the destruction of all joy and technology in society.
The result of this way of thinking, according to Rand, is that work
becomes oppressive and ruins the lives of those conscripted to it.
Rand calls this kind of work slavery and believes that it stifles all creativity and happiness. After this encounter with the World Council
of Scholars, Equality 7-2521 comes to realize that work must be
done for its own sake or because it benefits the individual, not
because it can be of any assistance to society.

4.   "I am. I think. I will."

Equality 7-2521 utters these words after he discovers the word "I" in Chapter XI. After proceeding through all his life using the word "we" to refer to himself, for the first time he experiences freedom and the joy that accompanies it. Once he is able to express himself using his new word, Equality 7-2521 is able to imagine a whole new life for himself and the Golden One, in which they live on their own land and eat food they produce. Rand believes the "I" must be the primary thought of the individual, while the "we" can be a second thought, at best. When the two are reversed, society becomes oppressive rather than liberating for men, and the dystopian world presented in *Anthem* comes into being. When the "I" is allowed to maintain its primacy, the world has beauty because the individual sees it and has meaning because the individual wills it. An individual who realizes his or her own self-worth lives only for him- or herself and for the "I" Equality 7-2521 first expresses here.

5.   But I still wonder how it was possible, in those
      graceless years of transition, long ago, that men did
      not see whither they were going, and went on, in
      blindness and cowardice, to their fate.

Part of the exposition of Equality 7-2521's newfound philosophy in
Chapter XII, these words describe his reflection on the history of the
human race and on how it came to disintegrate into madness and
fear through the evils of collectivism. *Anthem* is, above all else, a
political work, aimed at reforming those who have fallen to what
Rand believes is the collectivist heresy, and at giving comfort to those
who are still fighting for individualism. Rand believes that individualism will never actually perish because it is ingrained in human
existence; it is the root of man's happiness. Nevertheless, she thinks,
it is possible for man to lose sight of the importance of the ego and
allow society to become oppressive. *Anthem* is a wake-up call to
those who may be losing sight, and the "graceless years of transition" are supposed to be the years of its publication, when Rand sees
communism as taking hold not only in Russia but in the United
States as well.

KEY FACTS

FULL TITLE
Anthem

AUTHOR
Ayn Rand

TYPE OF WORK
Novella

GENRE
Dystopia; manifesto

LANGUAGE
English

TIME AND PLACE WRITTEN
The United States, 1937

DATE OF FIRST PUBLICATION
British edition, 1938; American edition, 1946

PUBLISHER
Signet

NARRATOR
Equality 7-2521 writes the journal of the events as they
transpire over the course of several months.

POINT OF VIEW
Equality 7-2521 speaks in the first person, writing in his journal
as the events transpire. He relates some of the conversations
verbatim, and other events he describes only from his own
perspective. He occasionally remarks on what other characters
are thinking.

TONE
Equality 7-2521 records his thoughts and actions in a
straightforward manner, with no trace of irony.

TENSE
Present, with some past-tense narration

SETTING (TIME)

In the future, after the collapse of the social order because of the common acceptance of collectivist values

SETTING (PLACE)

An unidentified city; much of the first half of *Anthem* is narrated from a tunnel underground where Equality 7-2521 is hiding, and the second half is narrated from a forest where he has taken refuge from a society that hates him.

PROTAGONIST

Equality 7-2521

MAJOR CONFLICT

Equality 7-2521 struggles for self-identification in a society that has rejected individualism in favor of collectivism.

RISING ACTION

Equality 7-2521 discovers a tunnel in which he begins hiding regularly to conduct scientific experiments; he invents the lightbulb; he decides to share his invention with the World Council of Scholars, even though he knows the way he came to discover electricity is illegal and sinful.

CLIMAX

Equality 7-2521's presentation of the lightbulb to the World Council permanently severs him from society and forces him out onto his own.

FALLING ACTION

Equality 7-2521 and the Golden One pursue their own lives together in the forest; they discover the meaning of individualism and the word "I."

THEMES

The primacy of the individual; the value of martyrdom; the impotence of the collective; original creation as a component of identity

MOTIFS

Fear; naming; shapelessness

SYMBOLS

Light; the forest; manuscripts

FORESHADOWING

The death of the Transgressor of the Unspeakable Word foreshadows the torture and exile of Equality 7-2521 and his ultimate epiphany upon discovering the word "I"; Equality 7-2521's growing obsession with the Uncharted Forest foreshadows his exile there; Equality 7-2521's torture at the hands of the Home Council foreshadows his exile by the World Council; The Golden One's attempts to say "I love you" foreshadow the epiphany of her discovery of the word "I."

STUDY QUESTIONS & ESSAY TOPICS

STUDY QUESTIONS

1. *What is the significance of nature in* Anthem? *Why does Equality 7-2521 flee to the forest when he is exiled from society?*

Nature represents the original and uncorrupted state of man in *Anthem*. Equality 7-2521 runs to the Uncharted Forest when he is exiled from society because there he is able to establish his freedom and start his life over as a new man. In society, Equality 7-2521 is unable to realize his potential because he is drawn down by the weaker members of society, who fear his strength and try to turn it against him. In nature, by contrast, he lives by the effort of his own hands and mind. The forest gives him what is rightly his, which includes all nature has to offer since man is the master and center of the universe.

In addition to representing a chance to start over, the forest represents a gateway into the past that society has lost but that Equality 7-2521 seeks. In the forest, he finds remnants of the world that disintegrated under the force of collectivism and has now all but disappeared. When he finds his home, he finds a key to that past, which the forest has preserved for him against the neglect of his collectivist society. The library provides him with information about the world that was, and, in fact, teaches him the word "I," which proves to be the trigger of his epiphanic self-realization. Thus, the forest offers Equality 7-2521 a way to go both forward by starting over on his own and back by connecting with the ideal society that existed before.

2.   *What is the significance of the story of the Transgressor*
      of the Unspeakable Word? What is the role of martyrdom
      in Anthem?

The Transgressor of the Unspeakable Word and Equality 7-2521 both suffer for what they believe in. In the case of the Transgressor of the Unspeakable Word, he burns at the stake for professing the word "I," the word it is not permitted in his society to say. In the case of Equality 7-2521, he is flogged for refusing to reveal his secret tunnel and, later, he is exiled for seeking solitude and pursuing scientific studies. The two are connected in two ways. First, the Transgressor of the Unspeakable Word seeks out Equality 7-2521 while he is being burned alive and smiles at him while he dies. Equality 7-2521 believes this event signifies a bond between the two men. Second, though society tortures both men physically, neither one suffers emotionally during the torture because they are glad to suffer for their ideal. For Rand, suffering of the body means nothing when it is endured in the name of an ideal.

Consistent with *Anthem*'s status as a political manifesto, Rand also makes reference to those she considers martyrs in the real-life battle against the evils of collectivist society. During his final exposition of his new philosophy, Equality 7-2521 addresses all the martyrs of the transition period, those who died for individualism while the world was just being converted to collectivism. These people are stand-ins for Rand's contemporaries, and the whole novella is meant as a way of reaching out to them and telling them that even though they suffer, they do so for an ideal that is worth suffering for and that will never die.

3.   *What is the setting of* Anthem? *Why does Rand not specify the story's time or location?*

Strictly speaking, the setting of *Anthem* is unclear. Rand reveals that it has been many years since the fall of the novella's society to collectivist ideals, but we do not know how many years. Moreover, it has been few enough years that the clothes in the closet at Equality 7-2521's new home in the forest are still intact. Similarly, the city in which the first part of the action occurs is unnamed, and the location of the Uncharted Forest is likewise unspecified. Rand employs this vagueness to make *Anthem* universal. She wants the novella to be a warning to all people everywhere that collectivism is an evil perpetrated on the human race, and that wherever it is implemented, it will bring about the demise of men. By not naming the city or the time, she leaves open the questions of where and how and when the collapse she foresees will happen.

In addition to the setting's vagueness making *Anthem* a sort of every-place warning, it also distances Rand from Soviet Russia in meaningful ways. Though details of the story unquestionably refer to the conditions in Russia under Lenin and Stalin, Rand is careful not to make *Anthem* explicitly about Russia because she wants to be clear that the evil of collectivism is not related only to the corruption of particular leaders and their henchmen. In this way, she answers the criticism of those who believe that Communism failed in Russia only because of specific historical conditions such as the cruelty of Stalin. Thus, the vagueness of the setting results in a deeper criticism of socialism than Rand could have achieved by making the story a concrete critique of a specific example of communism.

SUGGESTED ESSAY TOPICS

1. What is the significance of Rand's use of contrasted pairs in her imagery and her characters? For Rand, which is preferable, the dark and hard or the light and soft?

2. What is the role of the Golden One and International 4-8818 in the novella? How do they contribute to our understanding of Equality 7-2521 and the society around him?

3. How does the story of the life of Christ inform the story of Equality 7-2521? What role does religion play generally in objectivism?

4. What is Rand's view of women? Does the Golden One fit Rand's view of the individual who knows his or her self-worth?

5. What is the effect of the use of the word "we," and why is it important that the last chapter is the only place where the word "I" exists in the novella?

REVIEW & RESOURCES

QUIZ

1. Who is International 4-8818?

    A. The Golden One's father
    B. A member of the World Council of Scholars
    C. Equality 7-2521's best friend
    D. One of the screamers at the Home of the Students

2. Where does Equality 7-2521 write the beginning part of the novella?

    A. In a cave
    B. In a tunnel
    C. At his house
    D. On the street

3. What does the Golden One do for a living?

    A. She is a scholar
    B. She is a street sweeper
    C. She is a cook
    D. She is a peasant

4. Why do the members of the World Council of Scholars reject the lightbulb?

    A. Because they are afraid of it
    B. Because the bulb doesn't work
    C. Because they already have one
    D. Because the bulb is too bright

5. Why does Equality 7-2521 decide to offer the World
    Council of Scholars the lightbulb?

    A. He wants to help his brothers
    B. He wants the World Council of Scholars to forgive
        him for not telling the Home Council where he
        had been
    C. He wants the World Council of Scholars to pay him
        for his invention
    D. He wants to barter the lightbulb for a date with the
        Golden One

6. Where does Equality 7-2521 meet the Golden One?

    A. In the Palace of Mating
    B. At the World Council of Scholars
    C. In the field
    D. At the Home of Students

7. What word doesn't the Golden One know until the end of
    the novella?

    A. "You"
    B. "Them"
    C. "We"
    D. "I"

8. What does Equality 7-2521 do for a living, officially?

    A. He sweeps the streets
    B. He invents things
    C. He builds houses
    D. He fights for equality

9. Who is Prometheus?

    A. The Roman god of fire
    B. The Golden One
    C. The man who stole fire from the gods
    D. The god of the underworld

10. At the end of the novella, Equality 7-2521 does *not* plan to do which of the following?

    A. Kill Collective 0-0009
    B. Save International 4-8818
    C. Put up wire around his house
    D. Raise his son as a man

11. The first time they meet, what does Equality 7-2521 say to the Golden One?

    A. "What is your name?"
    B. "Dearest one . . ."
    C. "We love you."
    D. Nothing

12. What does Equality 7-2521 believe is the most important concept known to man?

    A. Light
    B. Ego
    C. Privacy
    D. Silence

13. Why does Equality 7-2521 break out of the Palace of Corrective Detention?

    A. The World Council is meeting
    B. He is being tortured
    C. The Golden One needs him
    D. He wants to work on his inventions

14. When does the story take place?

    A. 1984
    B. 2015
    C. 1917
    D. The year is unspecified

15. How does Equality 7-2521 escape the Palace of Corrective Detention?

    A. He threatens not to give the World Council the lightbulb
    B. He tunnels out
    C. He steals the keys
    D. He kicks the door down

16. Where does the story take place?

    A. New York
    B. Poland
    C. Russia
    D. The location is unspecified

17. What is the name of Ayn Rand's philosophy?

    A. Objectivism
    B. Subjectivism
    C. Collectivism
    D. Socialism

18. Equality 7-2521 discovers which of the following?

    A. Lightning
    B. Electricity
    C. Subatomic particles
    D. Greek manuscripts

19. Why don't the students talk to each other?

    A. They don't have anything to say
    B. They are not allowed
    C. They are afraid that the others might not agree with what they say
    D. They know they already agree

20. Who built the house in which Equality 7-2521 and the Golden One live at the end of the novella?

    A. The Homebuilders
    B. The Golden One
    C. Equality 7-2521
    D. Men from the Unmentionable Times

21. Why does Equality 7-2521 get sent to the Palace of Corrective Detention?

    A. For refusing to tell the Home Council where he was one night
    B. For inventing the lightbulb
    C. For talking to the Golden One
    D. For drinking out of the wrong water fountain

22. How does Equality 7-2521 discover electricity?

    A. In a thunderstorm
    B. By sticking his finger in a socket
    C. While dissecting a frog hanging on a copper wire
    D. The Golden One tells him about it

23. Of whom does Equality 7-2521 consider himself a disciple?

    A. The Golden One
    B. Jesus Christ
    C. Collective 0-0009
    D. The Transgressor of the Unspeakable Word

24. Where does Equality 7-2521 go when he is exiled?

    A. The tunnel
    B. The Palace of Corrective Detention
    C. The forest
    D. His new house

25. What is the most evil word in the language (according to Rand)?

   A. "I"
   B. "You"
   C. "We"
   D. "They"

ANSWER KEY:
1: C; 2: B; 3: D; 4: A; 5: A; 6: C; 7: D; 8: A; 9: C; 10: A;
11: D; 12: B; 13: A; 14: D; 15: D; 16: D; 17: A; 18: B; 19: C;
20: D; 21: A; 22: C; 23: D; 24: D; 25: C

SUGGESTIONS FOR FURTHER READING

ELLIS, ALBERT. *Is Objectivism a Religion?* New York: L. Stuart, 1968.

GOTTHELF, ALLAN. *On Ayn Rand.* Belmont, California: Wadsworth/Thomson Learning, 2000.

KELLEY, DAVID. *The Contested Legacy of Ayn Rand: Truth and Toleration in Objectivism.* Poughkeepsie, New York: Objectivist Center, 2000.

MERRILL, RONALD. *The Ideas of Ayn Rand.* La Salle, Illinois: Open Court, 1991.

PEIKOFF, LEONARD. *Objectivism: The Philosophy of Ayn Rand.* New York: Dutton, 1991.

ROBBINS, JOHN W. *Answer to Ayn Rand: A Critique of the Philosophy of Objectivism.* Washington, D.C.: Mount Vernon Publishing Company, 1974.

SCIABARRA, CHRIS MATTHEW. *Ayn Rand: The Russian Radical.* University Park, Pennsylvania: Pennsylvania State University Press, 1995.

SparkNotes Study Guides:

SPARKNOTES TEST PREPARATION GUIDES

The SparkNotes team figured it was time to cut standardized tests down to size. We've studied the tests for you, so that SparkNotes test prep guides are:

Smarter:
Packed with critical-thinking skills and test-taking strategies that will improve your score.

Better:
Fully up to date, covering all new features of the tests, with study tips on every type of question.

Faster:
Our books cover exactly what you need to know for the test. No more, no less.